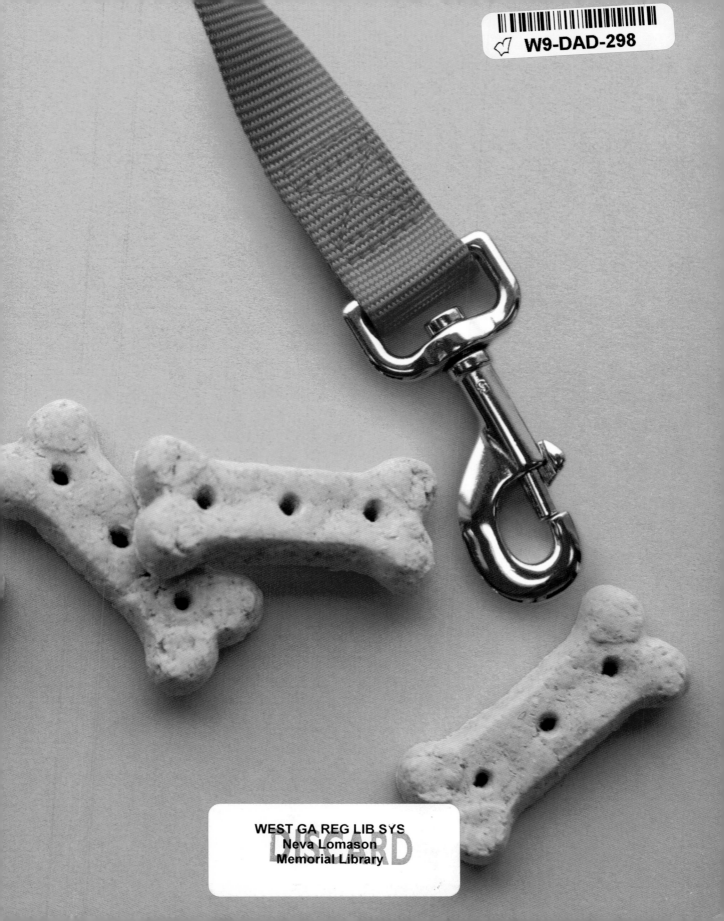

To our smart cookies, Rory and Tess. Always keep learning and dream BIG!
Love, Mom and Dad

A NOTE ABOUT THE POEMS

Dog-Gone School features a number of fun poetic forms. They are:
acrostic ("R.E.A.D.," p. 27), **cinquain** ("Masterpiece," p. 25),
climbing rhyme ("Book Nook," p. 8), **couplet** ("Unleashed," p. 17),
doggerel ("Home Free," pp. 28–31), **free verse** ("Globetrotting," p. 20),
haiku ("Lab Work," p. 7), **math poem** ("Adding Up," p. 6),
monorhyme ("Teacher's Pet," p. 5, and "Spellbound," p. 19),
onomatopoeia ("SLURP!," pp. 10–11, and "Tuning Up," p. 12), and
quatrain (untitled, p. 3, "Lunch Bunch," pp. 14–15, and "Not Me," p. 22).

Text copyright © 2013 by Amy Schmidt
Jacket and interior photographs copyright © 2013 by Ron Schmidt

Visit us on the Web! randomhouse.com/kids

Educators and librarians, for a variety of teaching tools, visit us at RHTeachersLibrarians.com

Library of Congress Cataloging-in-Publication Data
Schmidt, Amy.
Dog-gone school / by Amy Schmidt ; photographs by Ron Schmidt. — 1st ed.
pages cm.
ISBN 978-0-375-86974-7 (trade) — ISBN 978-0-375-96974-4 (lib. bdg.) —
ISBN 978-0-375-98538-6 (ebook)
1. School—Juvenile poetry. 2. Dogs—Pictorial works. I. Schmidt, Ron, photographer. II. Title.
PS3619.C4453 D64 2013 811'.6—dc23 2012047331

MANUFACTURED IN CHINA

10 9 8 7 6 5 4 3 2 1

First Edition

DOG-GONE SCHOOL

Poems by
Amy Schmidt

Photographs by
Ron Schmidt

Random House 🏠 New York

Hop on the bus.
No time to wait!
It's time for school.
We can't be late!

Teacher's Pet

This is Lucy.
She never is tardy, on that you can bet.
She perfectly recites the alphabet.
She never makes the teacher upset.
And she is as helpful as one can get.
That's why Lucy is the teacher's pet.

Adding Up

If Simon lost 2 blocks
And then he lost 2 more,
How many blocks would be lost?
The answer would be 4!

Maybe he should check the floor!

Lab Work

Mix, measure, pour, weigh.
In class, I'm a scientist
Experimenting.

Book Nook

Shelves of books,
Reading nooks,
Authors, narrators,
And illustrators.
Tales of knights and fairy tales,
Facts on mummies, bats, or whales!
So many stories all in one space.
Check out what they have in this cool place!

SLURP!

Ralphie has a hallway pass
To visit the water fountain.
He can't reach to get a drink,
So he's built a giant mountain.
Slurp
Slurp
Hiccup
Slurp
Slurp
Slurp
Hiccup

Burp!

10

With a belly full of water,
Ralphie sloshes back to class.
But on his way, he starts to think
He'll need a bathroom pass!

Tuning Up

The saxophone wails.
The tuba bellows.
The flute lets out a tweet.

The trumpet whines.
The cymbals crash.
The drum keeps steady beat.

Abuzz with harmony.

Lunch Bunch

MILK

Open   SELL BY

Ultra-Pasteurized   HALF PINT (250mL)

We should be eating lunch right now,
But we just sit and stare.
All we see are homemade cookies
And hope that he will share!

Unleashed

Bell is ringing. It's midday.
Recess! Hooray! Time to play!
Swinging feet fly toward the sky.
A game of tag starts close by.
Zooming down the giant slide.
Someone's seeking . . . run and hide!
Squealing, laughing girls and boys,
Monkey bars and springy toys,
Jump rope, hopscotch,
    games with friends.
Bell is ringing. Recess ends.

Spellbound

Maddie has a word that she is working hard to spell.
It's a very common word, one Maddie knows quite well.
Is the letter that she needs a *B* or *C* or *L*?
If you know the missing letter, go ahead and tell!

Globetrotting

At our school,
On our street,
In our city,
Inside our state,
Within our country,
On our continent,
Of this world.

Not Me

We don't know how it started,
And they won't tell us who,
But one of these two fellows
Chewed up their teacher's shoe.

PRINCIPAL

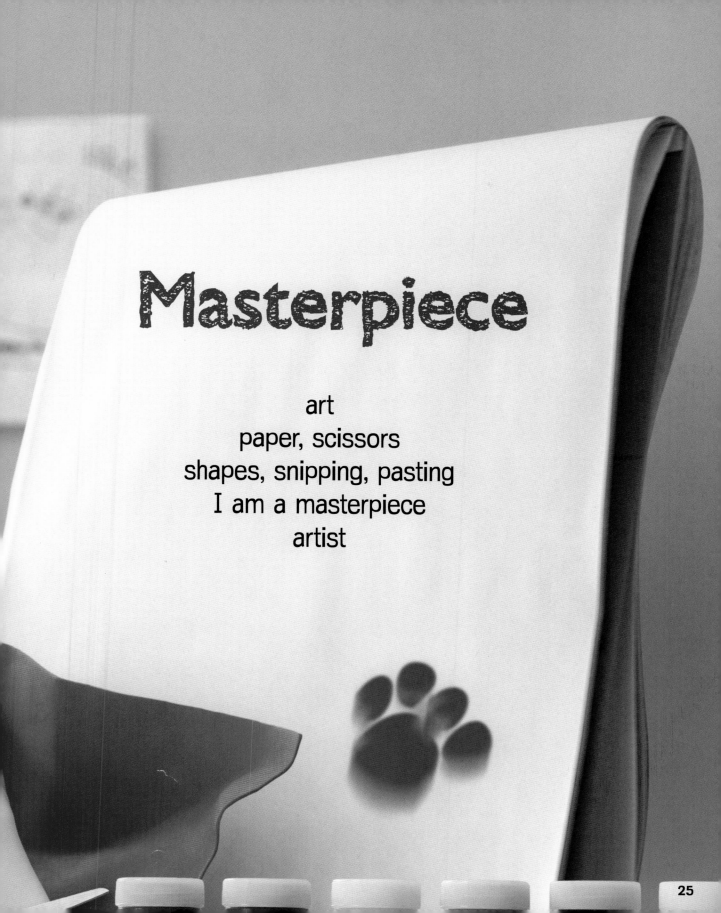

Masterpiece

art
paper, scissors
shapes, snipping, pasting
I am a masterpiece
artist

R.E.A.D.

Racing to the shelf,
Ellie picked a special book
And settled down in a favorite spot to
Dig into a good story.

Home Free

The bell has rung
To end the day.
Gather your things.
Head home to play. . . .

OMEWORK.
OMEWORK.
OMEWORK.
OMEWORK.
HOMEWORK.

OMEWORK.
OMEWORK.
OMEWORK.
MEWORK.
OMEWORK.

OMEWORK.
OMEWORK.
HOMEWORK.
OMEWORK.
OMEWORK.
OMEWORK.
OMEWORK.

I WILL NOT EAT MY HOMEWORK.
I WILL NOT EAT MY HOMEWORK.
I WILL NOT EAT MY HOMEWORK.
I WILL NOT EAT MY HOMEWORK.
I WILL NOT EAT MY HOMEWORK.
I WILL NOT EAT MY HOMEWORK.
I WILL NOT EAT MY HOMEWORK.
I WILL NOT EAT MY HOMEWORK.
I WILL NOT EAT MY HOMEWORK.
I WILL NOT EAT MY HOMEWORK.
I WILL NOT EAT MY HOMEWORK.
I WILL NOT EAT MY HOMEWORK.
I WILL NOT EAT MY HOMEWORK.
I WILL NOT EAT MY HOMEWORK.
I WILL NOT EAT MY HOMEWORK.
I WILL NOT EAT MY HOMEWORK.
I WILL NOT EAT MY HOMEWORK.
I WILL NOT EAT MY HOMEWORK.

Except for Stan.
He has to stay.

Class Superlatives

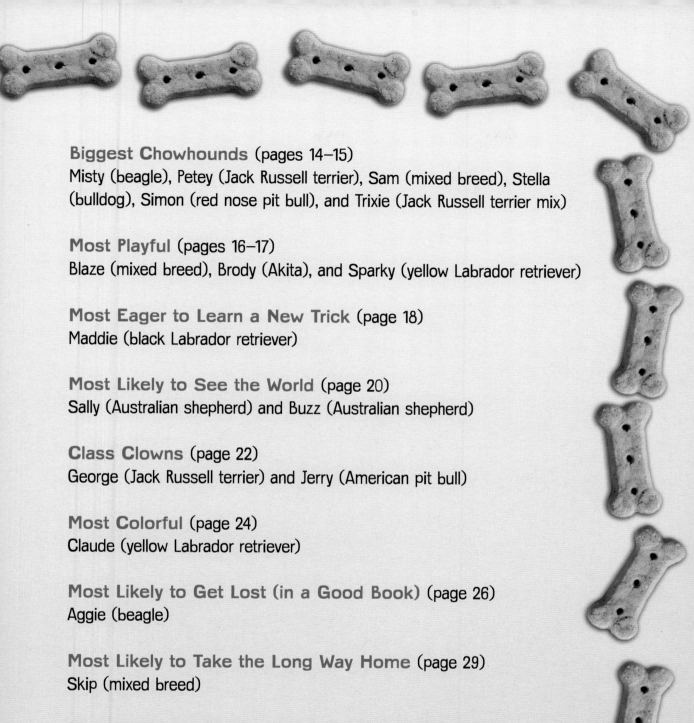

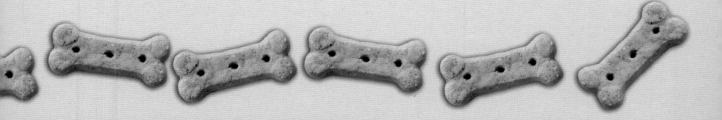